Murder, We Coloured

Fanart-based colouring book for fans and future fans of J.B. Fletcher & Co.!

Created with greatest gratitude and love for our beloved Angela Lansbury and one of her most iconic roles as J.B. Fletcher in the CBS hit series 'Murder, She Wrote'.

Join the community and share your colouring masterpieces by using #MurderWeColoured or #MurderWeColored on any of your preferred social media platforms.

Now enjoy and bike on!
All the best,
Sam, 2022

Introduction by Jenny Hammerton
author of 'Murder, She Cooked' and many more

Oh my! Grab your pencils or felt tips, serve yourself a big slice of Angela Lansbury's Walnut Date Bread and get cosy. Take a break from your busy life for some Cabot Cove colouring!

What will you choose first? There are many great scenes from Murder, She Wrote to select from within these pages. But, for me, it's got to be the split second when Edna is about to whack Jessica with her handbag in Sticks and Stones.

I plan to have that very episode playing in the background as I enjoy the soothing sound of pencil lead on paper. For the images featuring Tim Benzie on stage during a Solve-Along-A-Murder-She-Wrote™ event, I'll be reminiscing about the added fun he brings to the show. I'm not sure I'll be able to colour myself in, but maybe I'll give myself pink hair just for fun.

Thanks a million, Sam, for creating a fabulous way for us Fangelas to celebrate the show we all love. I'm looking forward to seeing some great works of colouring art popping up on social media. #MurderWeColoured #MurderWeColored

Inspired by 'The Murder of Sherlock Holmes'
Season 1, Episode 1
Drawn by @Niku30_

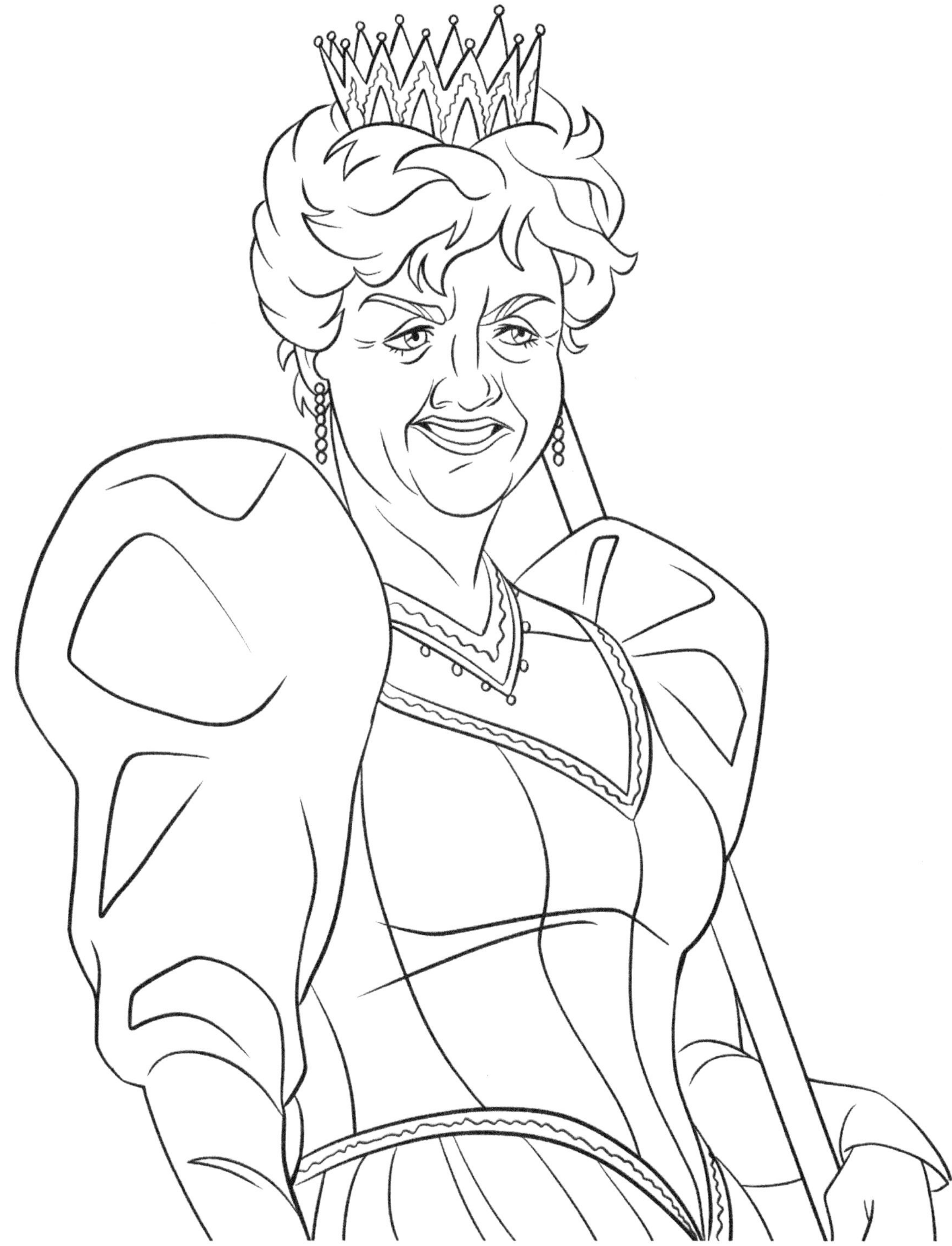

Season 4, Episode 12
Drawn by @Niku30_

Inspired by 'Who Threw the Barbitals in Mrs. Fletcher's Chowder?'
Season 4, Episode 12
Drawn by @Niku30_

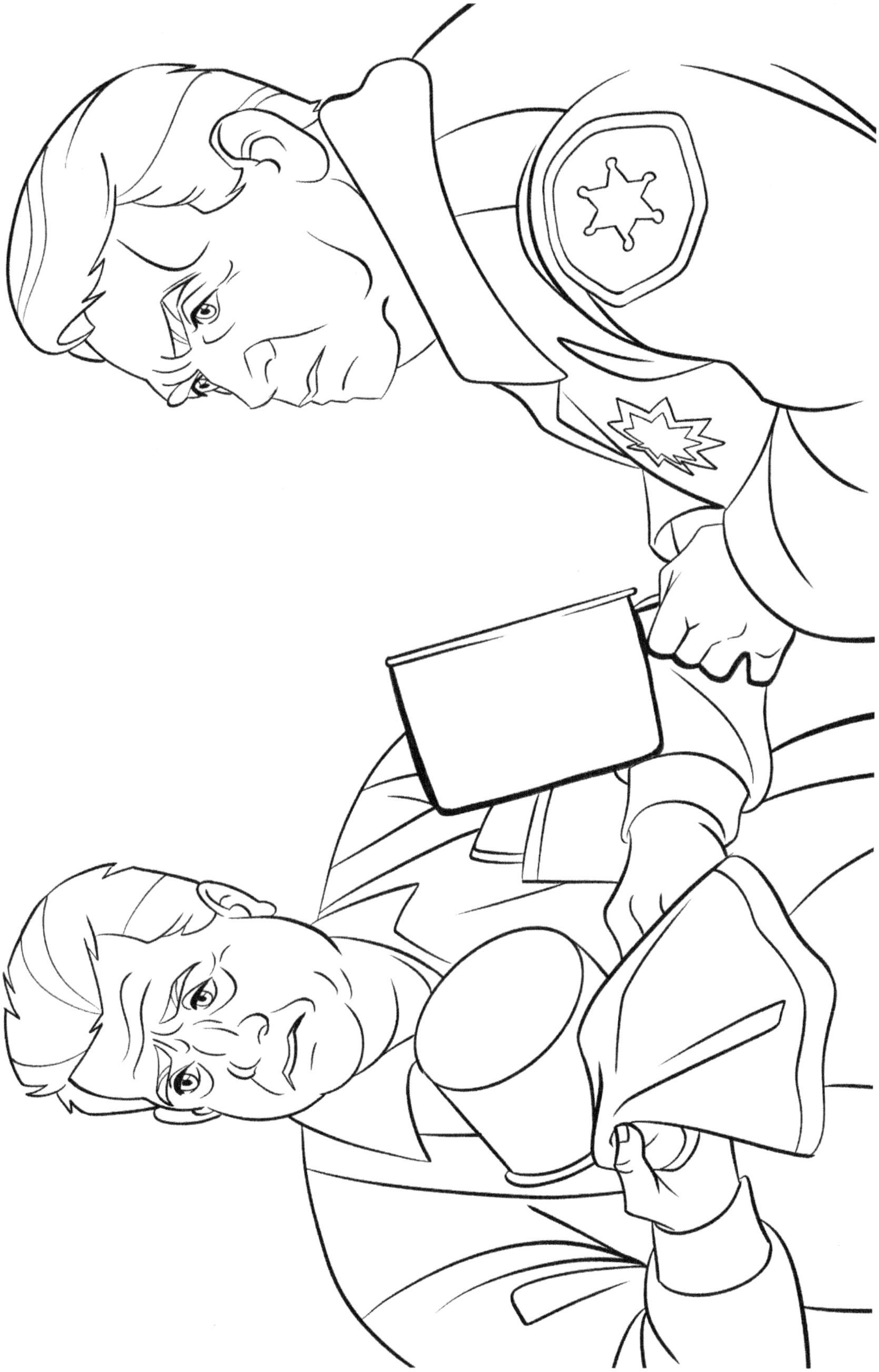

Inspired by 'Lovers and Other Killers'
Season 1, Episode 5

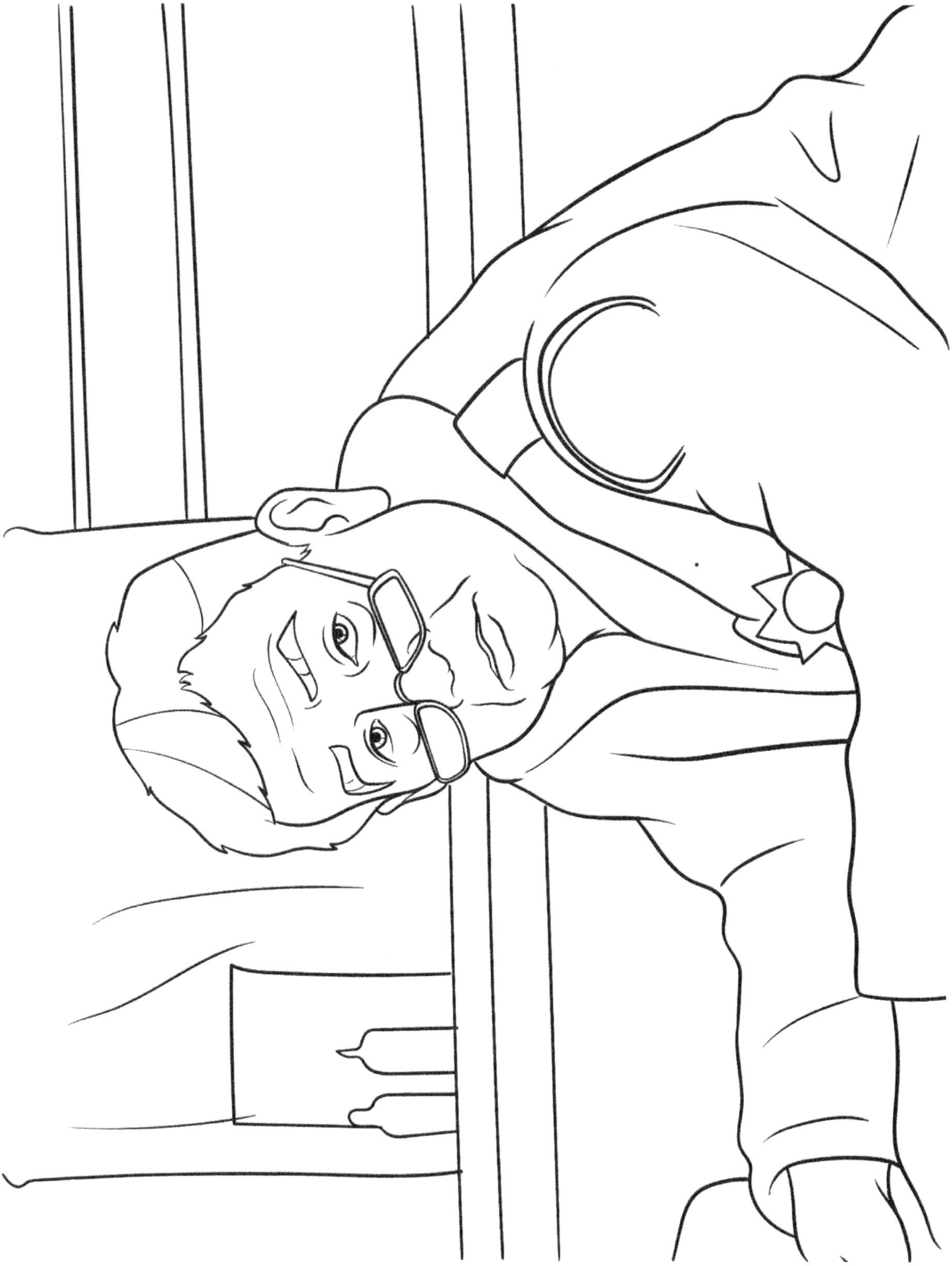

Inspired by 'Birds of a Feather'
Season 1, Episode 2

Inspired by 'My Johnny Lies Over the Ocean'
Season 1, Episode 14

Inspired by 'Murder Takes the Bus'
Season 1, Episode 19

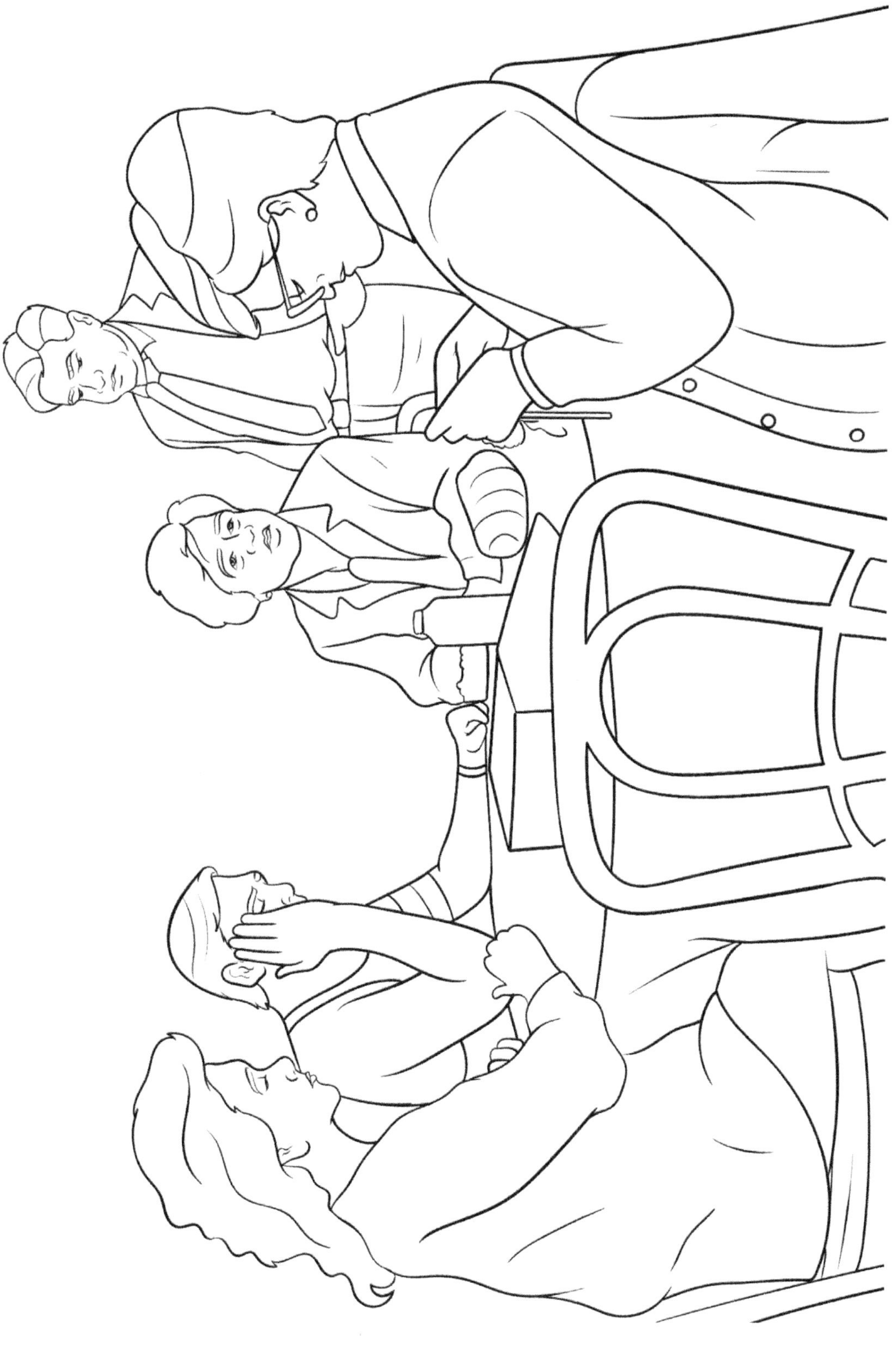

Inspired by Tim Benzie's 'Solve-Along-A-Murder-She-Wrote™'
https://www.instagram.com/solvealongamurdershewrote

Inspired by Tim Benzie's 'Solve-Along-A-Murder-She-Wrote™'
https://www.instagram.com/solvealongamurdershewrote

Solve-Along-A Murder She Wrote

Inspired by 'Sing a Song of Murder'
Season 2, Episode 5

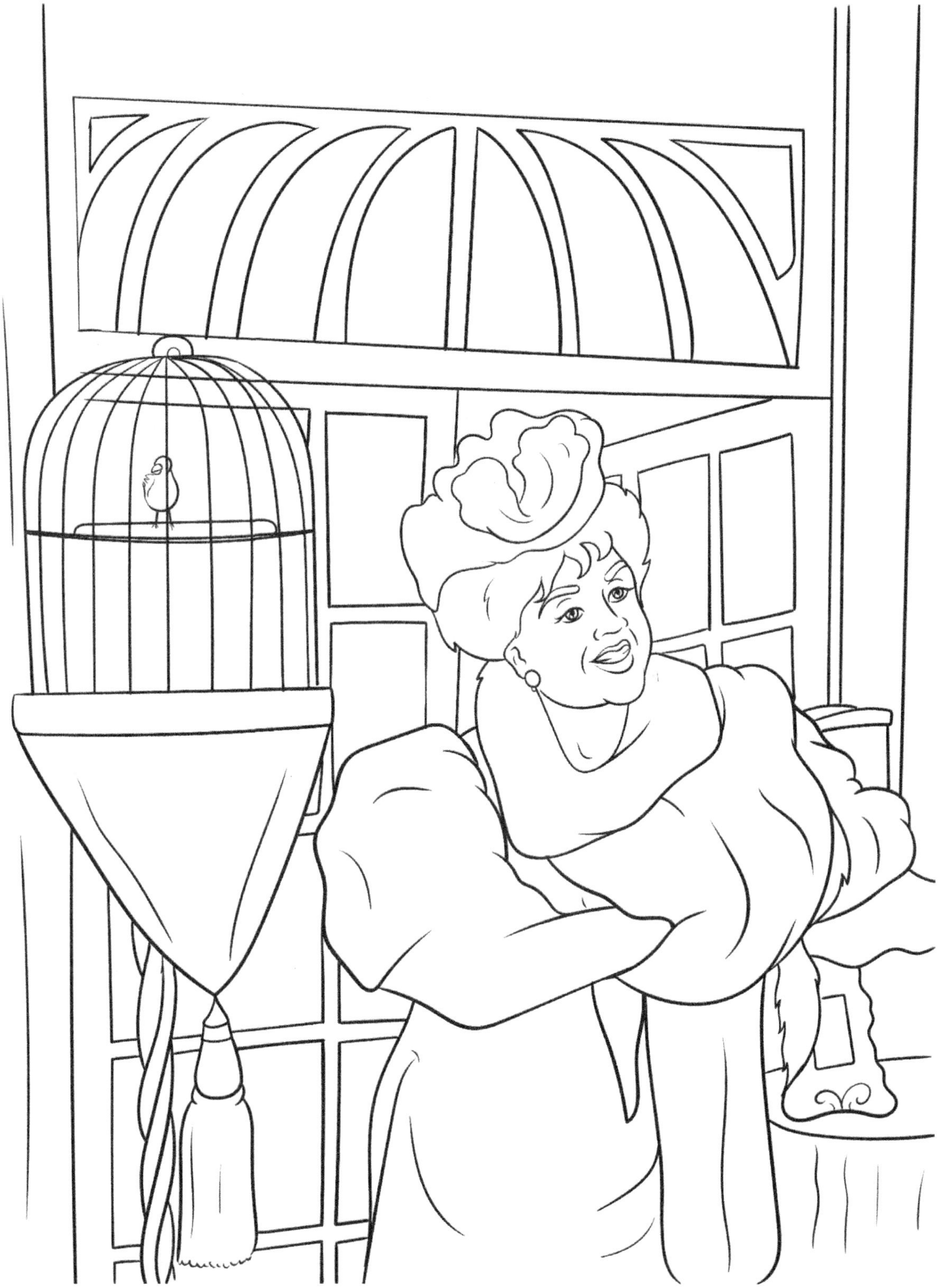

Inspired by 'Sing a Song of Murder'
Season 2, Episode 5

Inspired by 'Jessica Behind Bars'
Season 2, Episode 9

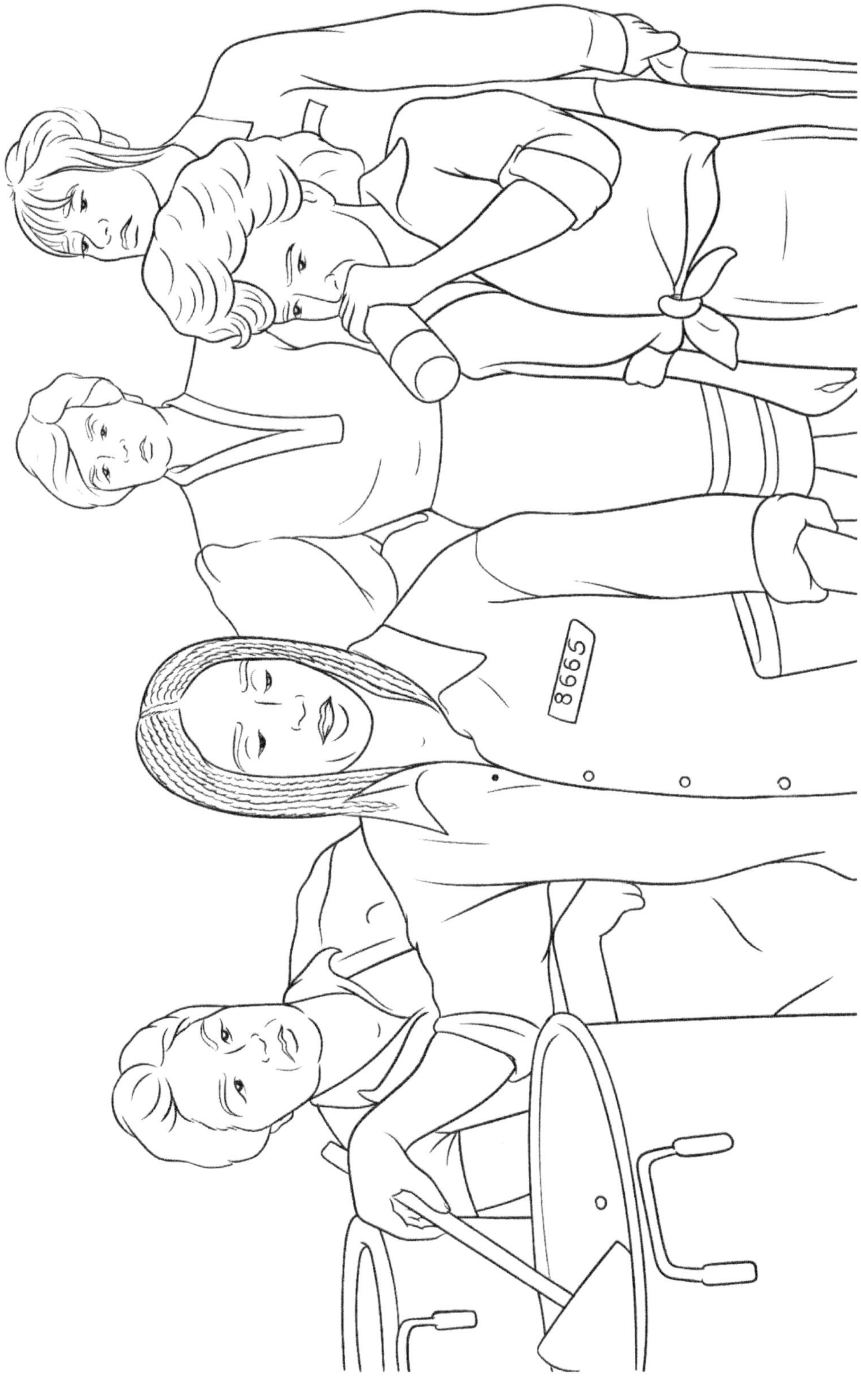
8665

Inspired by 'Sticks and Stones'
Season 2, Episode 10

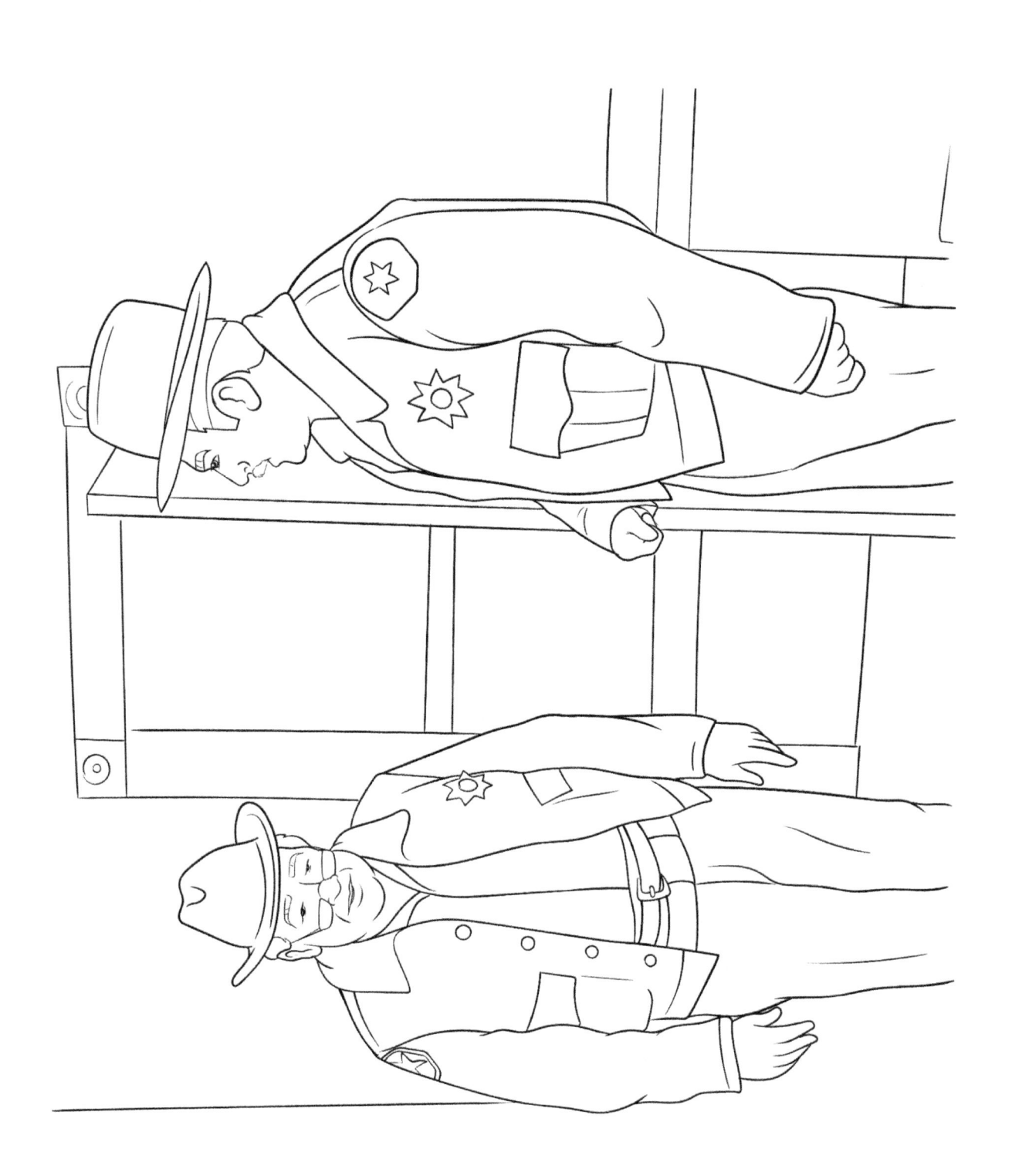

Inspired by 'Sticks and Stones'
Season 2, Episode 10

Inspired by 'Death Stalks the Big Top'
Season 3, Episode 1&2

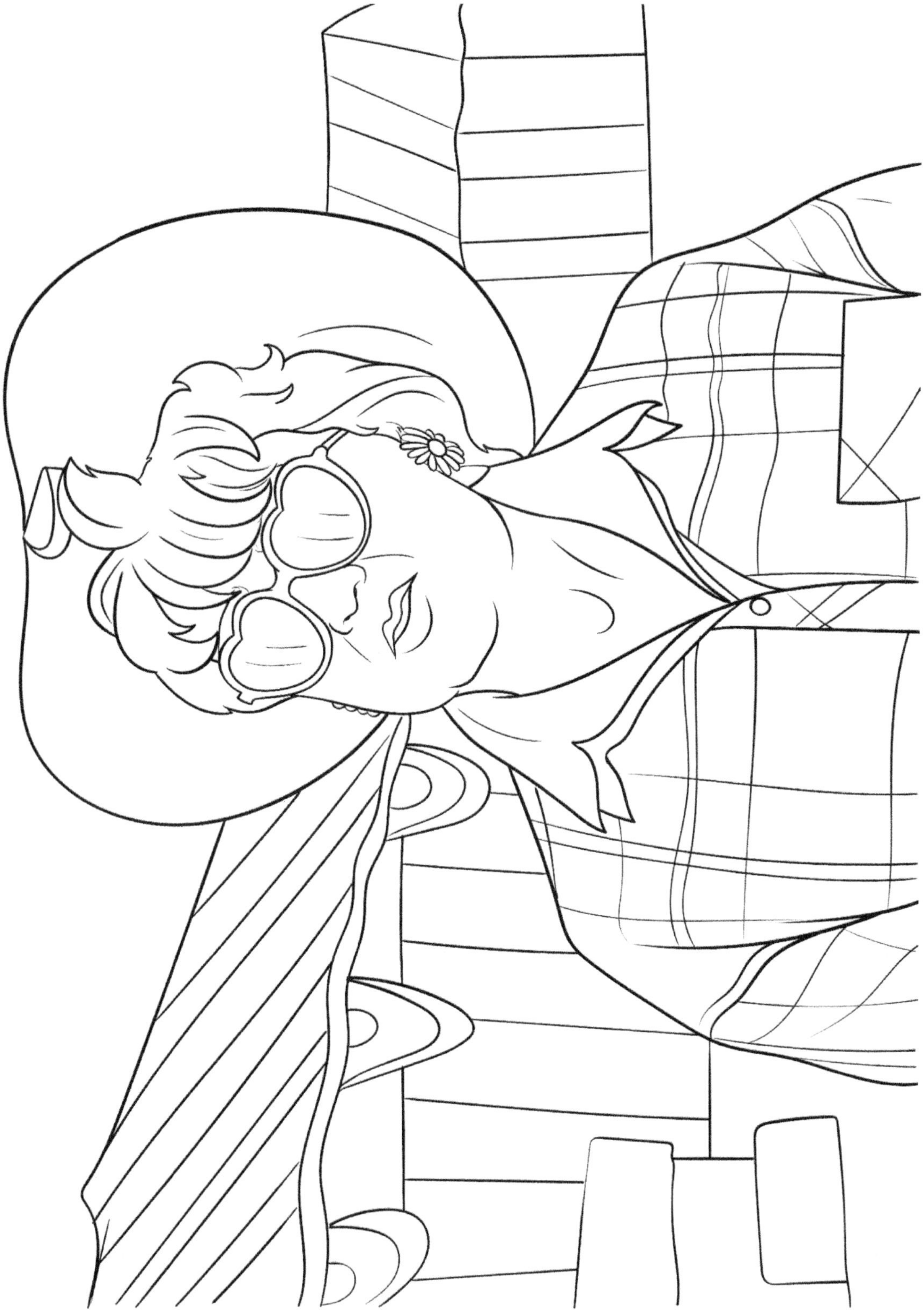

Inspired by 'If it's Thursday, It Must Be Beverly'
Season 4, Episode 7

Inspired by 'A Virtual Murder'
Season 10, Episode 5

12:00 WED   04/17/01

PLAYER 1 READY

Inspired by 'A Virtual Murder'
Season 10, Episode

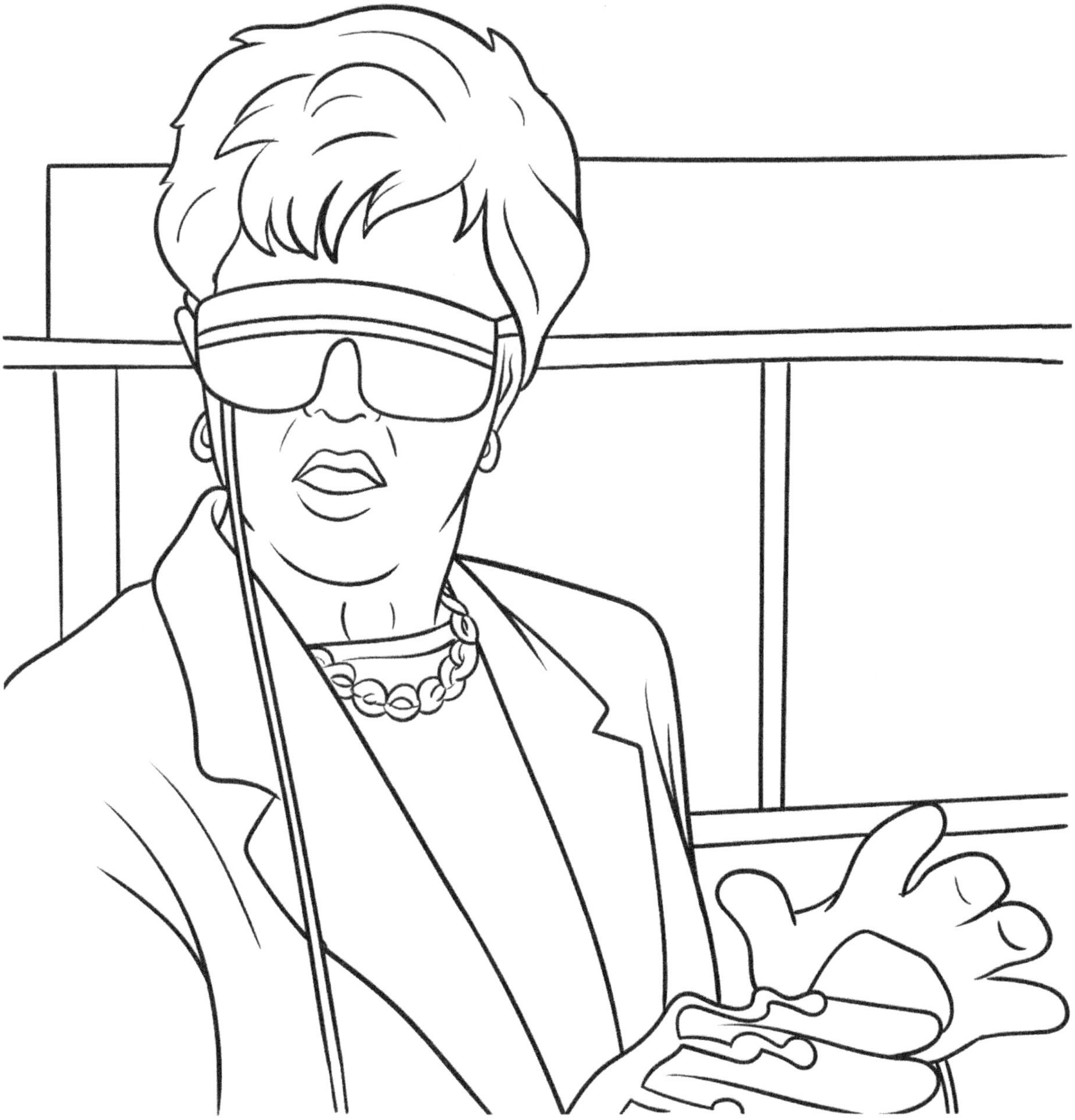

Inspired by a group promo picture

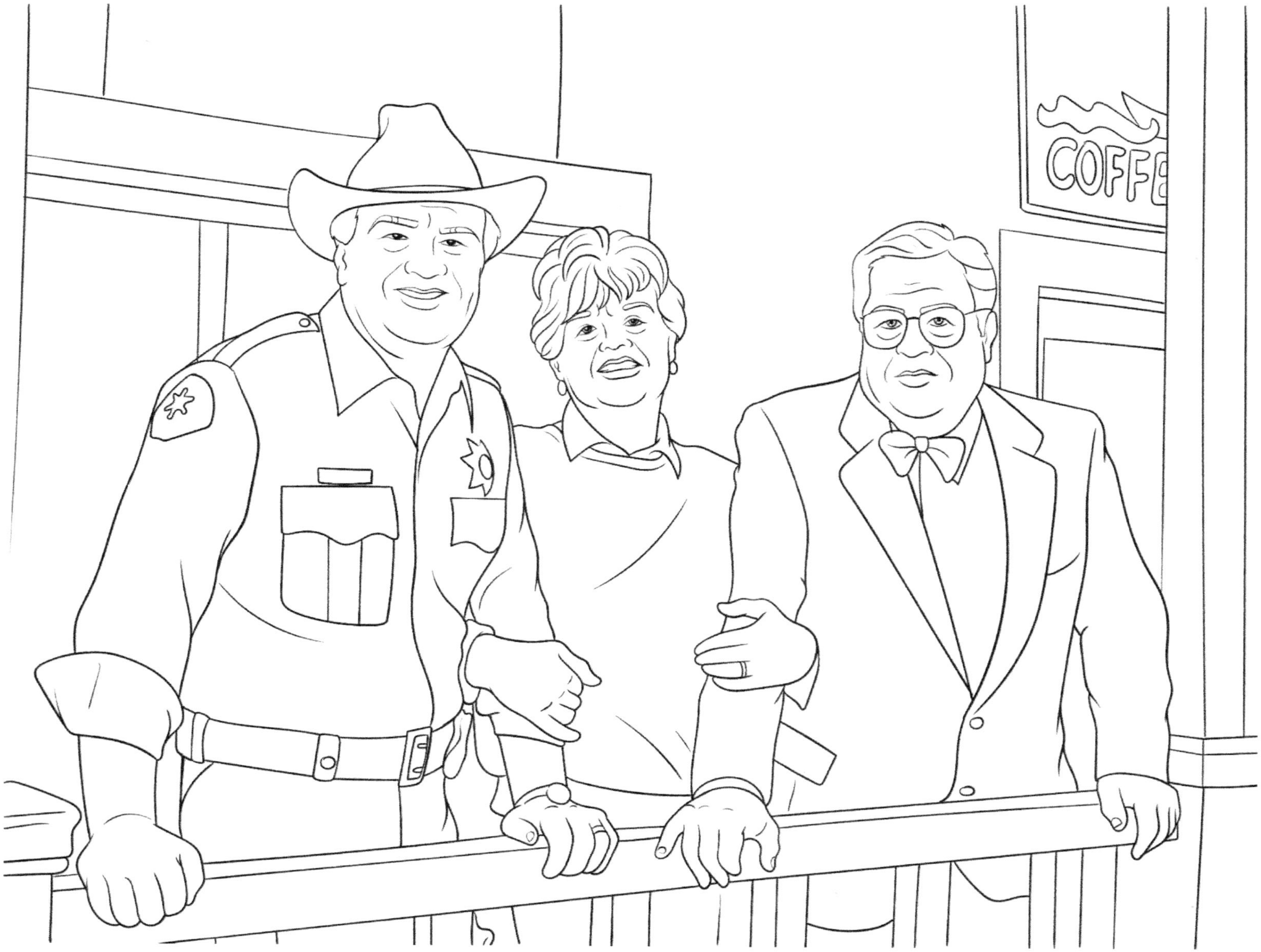
COFFE

Inspired by Jessica on her bike

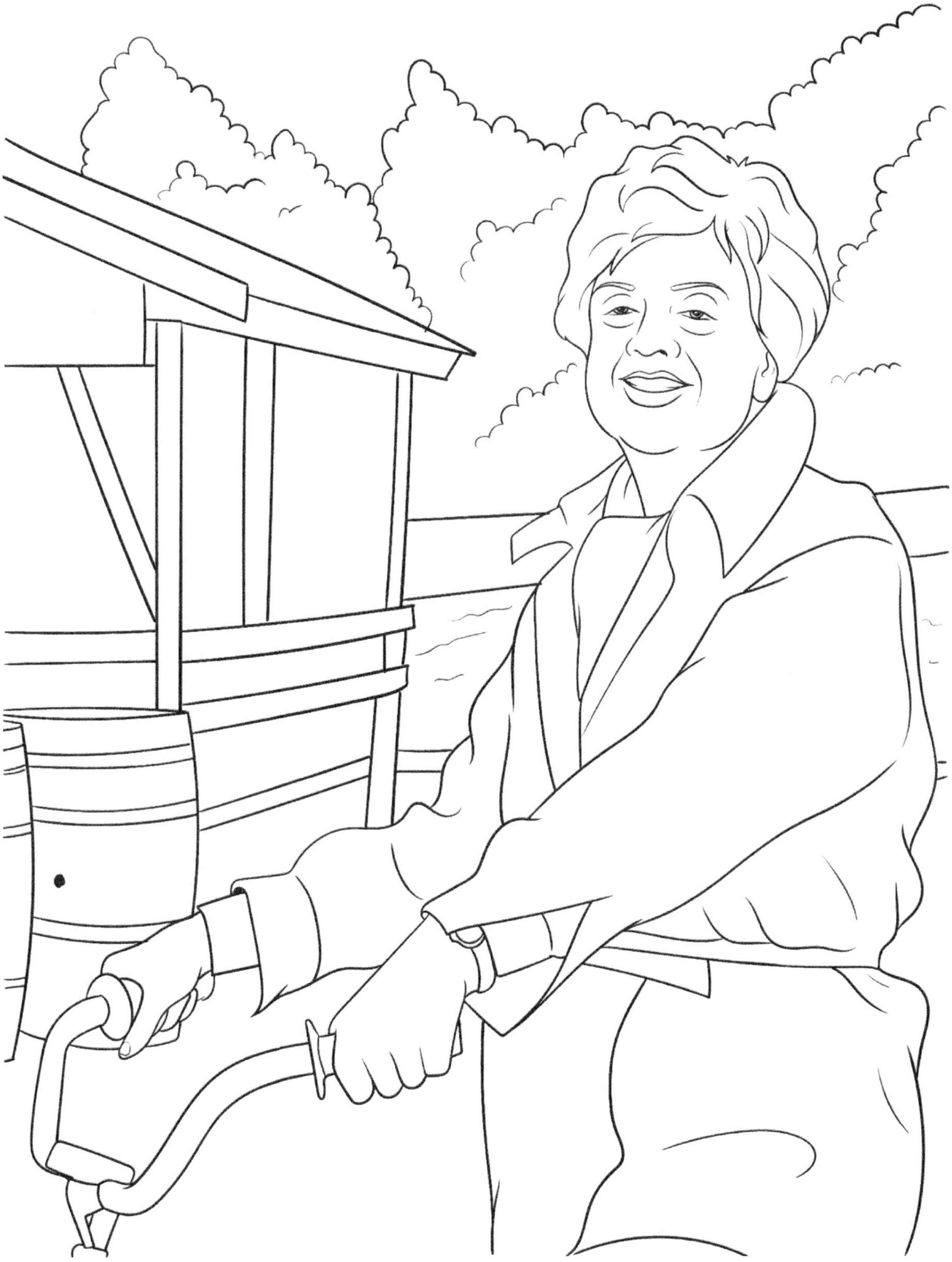

Inspired by 'Weave a Tangled Web'
Season 5, Episode 10

Inspired by a promo picture

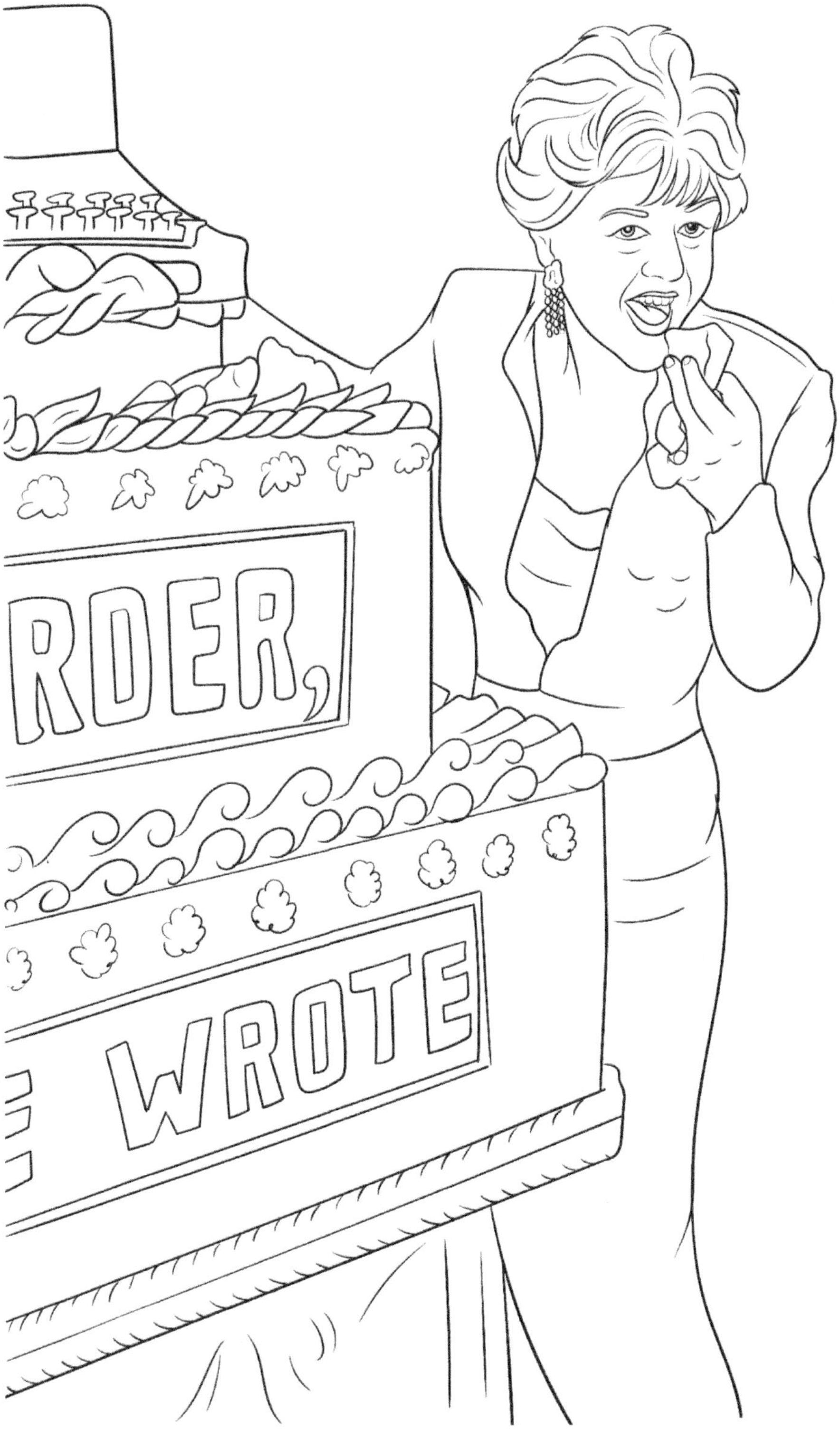
RDER,
WROTE

Special Thanks

Our special thanks go to Jenny Hammerton and Tim Benzie, who are a solid rock in the Murder, She Wrote fan base in and around the UK. While you can't blame them for the content or the creation of this colouring book, they did support us with kind words of encouragement as well as pictures of themselves for this book and for that we are very grateful!

Jenny Hammerton is a film archivist who just released another one of her TV show and movie based cook books '**Murder, She Cooked: A Cabot Cove Cookbook**' on **Amazon**. You can also find her very lively and always interesting blog here:
https://www.silverscreensuppers.com

Tim Benzie is the host of interactive screenings of the show and tours mainly through the UK but if you are lucky, you might catch him in Ireland or his home country Australia as well. To find out more about his amazingly funny show, check out:
https://solvealongamurdershewrote.com

Also a warm thank you to **Anna**, wife and editor extraordinaire.

If you enjoyed this passion project then please share your interpretations and creations by using **#MurderWeColoured** or **#MurderWeColored** on any social platforms of your liking!

Thank you very much for your support by purchasing this fanart!

Stay safe and bike on (WWJBFD?),

Sam (creator of this book and obsessor of everything and everyone Murder, She Wrote)

Printed in Great Britain
by Amazon